A Dreamer's Mind

NIHARIKA BODLA

INDIA · SINGAPORE · MALAYSIA

ISBN
Paperback 979-8-89556-279-6
Hardcase 979-8-89588-916-9

The book depicts the story of a girl's life that is exposed
to societal pressures and overwhelming stigma. It shows
us her pain as she keeps a facade and hides her feelings
to maintain relationships, making an individual lose
their sense of identity.

[T.W. Attempted suicide]

Sick on my journey,
My dreams go wandering,
On this withered field.

– Matsuo Basho, Death Haiku

CONTENTS

PROLOGUE

A world of dew,

And within every dewdrop,

A world of struggle.

By Kobayashi Issa

She felt caged, with nothing left to wish for. Yet, here she was, enclosed by nothing but love, affection, and warmth. The sound of happiness echoed through the room. She felt the joy of her parents course through her veins. It was the perfect night. She got accepted into her honors program; her dad had gotten a promotion earlier that day, and the most delicious food was cooked to celebrate. She lived in a more-than-comfortable sized home, making it spacious yet homely and cozy at the same time. Cute family pictures lined the walls above the stairs that led to the second level of their house. They reinforced the ideal perception of a family such as theirs. Everyone who ever walked through those front doors never missed their chance to praise them: "Oh, what a lovely house you have," "Such a perfect family, how do you do it?" In reality, they weren't wrong. She was grateful for her position, the home and room she had, the love that surrounded her, her parents' acceptance of anything she went through or wanted, and the academic success that graced her in school. So, was it wrong for her to always feel so bad?

The aroma of lavender essential oil diffused through the air, bringing back memories of previous nights. Her family's evening was all about freshly made pasta and garlic bread, a half-finished bottle of wine, a tiny carton of apple juice for herself, soft music that played in the background, and fairy lights and cutely shaped candles illuminating them as they dined. Aleia's soul sank. Time and again, the chit-chat and laughter morphed into something she dreaded with every cell in her being. Her eyes teared up, clenching and unclenching her hands to ease the pain welling up in her heart.

Her mom's voice calmly broke through her thoughts. "Hey, are you okay, sweetie?" When the young girl stared up in confusion, panic dancing around her eyes, a frown appeared on her mother's face. "You've barely touched your food. You should eat some more."

That was the last trigger she needed before she broke down. To save herself from embarrassment, she hurriedly excused herself from the table and ran up to her room. Her door was locked, no windows or vents open, and she was surrounded by pitch black. Her body was wavering, unable to focus on any one object. In despair, she slid down against the wall as her vision blurred, and waves of pain emitted from her chest through her body.

"Not again, not again, not again." Her hands rapidly shook as she tried to calm herself down. She couldn't breathe. She couldn't stop her body from trembling as she gasped for air. Her arms desperately clutched her lungs through her sweat-soaked shirt. She sobbed, yet no tears left her eyes. She hopelessly screamed, but the sound never left her mouth. Nothing she heard was the same. The girl felt as though her head was being forced underwater, and all noise became muffled and foggy. Huddled in a corner, Aleia could feel the walls begin to close in on her, further cutting off her supply of oxygen and air. Her eyes darted across the room, hyperfocusing solely on the rapidly thumping heart in her chest, not noticing anything but the stinging pain in her wrists. Once the first drop of blood trickled down her arm, she could sense the circulation being cut off from her head, making her feel faint. The heavy breaths never ended, the pain never stopped, the silhouette of her room slowly faded away, and the world went black.

***

She was sixteen years old, studying in a high-end private school with little to no will to live. No one could know that, though, could they? They never did, and they never will. Her stupid problems began around two years ago, the day her mind turned on her. Growing up, she was raised to believe in the importance of equality, perseverance, and hard work. Her mother was a lawyer and a very good one, for that matter. She changed and protested multiple laws in their country (explicitly focusing on stopping the sexual harassment of women at work). She fought against an unjust society, making her mark and spreading hope in thousands of other women who wanted to see the light at the end of the tunnel. The struggles her mom went through made Aleia understand the number of corrupt ideals present in the world and the unfairness of simply being a person who doesn't align with the perspective of what society believes.

She realized the insignificance of her existence.

CHAPTER 1

A TRIP DOWN MEMORY LANE

A weathered skeleton
In windy fields of memory,
Piercing like a knife.

By Matsuo Basho.

AUGUST 16TH, 2014

It was the first day of eighth grade. She was so excited she could barely sleep the previous night. The eager 13-year-old got up before sunlight could hit the sky and started preparing her bag, snack, appearance, and a speech she made to be the friendliest girl around. It was nothing short of a perfect day. Fresh notebooks filled her bag, the weather was neither too hot nor too cold, the smell of dew and jasmine graced her, and the crisp wind played with the young girl, messing up the neat braid her mom did for her as she made her way to school. She hurriedly attempted to smooth out the loose strands of brown hair while walking the distance between the school gate and the building's entrance. The eager buzz of students echoed through the courtyard, making Aleia remember the true magic of 'first days.' Her perfectly labelled notebooks, packed snack box, full water bottle, and three packs of pens were neatly organised in the backpack she was currently hauling through the corridors of a place all-too-familiar to her. She greeted all the cleaning staff a good morning, frowning when she realized they never bothered hiring a male janitor.

She recollected the details she read about her teacher: her room number, name, experience, etc. After she vaguely remembered her mom telling her it was someone named "Mrs. Smith," room 202, Aleia made her way up two staircases. The young girl happily thought, *'The last year of freedom, huh? I better make the most of it then'*. She swung open the door to her new second home, promptly scanned the room for her seat and locker, and put her baggage away in the blink of an eye. After a warm welcome, a self-introduction to her classmates, and the creation of acquaintances that she prayed would last at least a month, the rest of the day felt like a surreal dream.

AUGUST 22ND, 2015

Adrenaline coursed through her veins as a new school began appearing behind the large oak trees. It was the beginning of a new chapter, and for the first time, her heart tugged her toward nervousness rather than excitement. She bid her mom farewell through the tinted car windows, faced the building in front of her, and took in all its beauty. A small village made for learning littered acres of land; tall buildings loomed over her, and a cobbled path was perfectly laid out, inciting her to take the first steps into a new phase of her life. Her brown and gold heterochromatic eyes darted around to comprehend the environment surrounding her. A few different groups of people were talking among themselves on the lawn, some sitting, some standing, and some reclining on the grass. Bright pink flowers littered the soil, some beginning to decompose and some that were freshly fallen. Clusters of first-year students stormed the school, making a beeline toward the two double glass doors that harshly glinted a block away from her.

She took a deep breath, muttered, *"Here we go again,"* sent a silent orison to whatever God believed in her, and began moving forward. Moments later, she was lost among the crowds. Her vision was obscured by the unruly stampede of high schoolers, her olfaction was overwhelmed with the abundance of cheap cologne wafting through the air, and she was truly surprised her ears had the ability to process this much sound without going deaf. With her mild claustrophobia and her being in this incredibly dense human mound, fainting was inevitable. The real question was *when*.

Aleia could hear her throbbing heart in her head as it beat rhythmically, pounding within the walls of her skull. She sluggishly made her way toward the open doors, with the new excitement of students echoing through the air. 'There it was,' she thought: the gateway to something she had never experienced. The second she stepped through those [slightly tinted, she discovered] double doors, a refreshing wall of cold air smacked her. It was at that moment that she decided she would never take her AC for granted again.

After the stampede settled down as the students dispersed into the various corridors of the school, Aleia found herself alone (well, alone if she disregarded the four arbitrary students brooding in the background). One hand tightly clutched the strap of her backpack, and the other squeezed a small rectangle of paper that had her timetable printed on it.

Sure, she was only fourteen, but at that point, she thought she could do something with her life. Call her airheaded and overconfident, but she felt ready to take on the future.

SEPTEMBER 1ST, 2016

Something melancholic was boiling in the pit of her stomach, and she was trying to figure out *what*. Unlike in previous years, she wasn't happy or nervous. Aleia was downright scared, but the reason never surfaced in her mind. She felt as though there was a ticking hourglass in her body, and the second the final grain fell, she would become numb. With shaky hands, she opened those tinted glass doors and was back in the same hallway. Underneath all her fear and anxiety, she had a twisted sense of comfort. What bothered her the most was why she had this irrational fear. Aleia was one of the most competent students in her grade; she had impressive extracurriculars and was almost all the teacher's pet (that was not a brag). The same moldy beige walls stared back at her, peeking behind the borders of lockers that lined it. The fluorescent white lights that line the ceiling gave a weird glow to everything beneath it, making it seem like she was the main character of a trashy horror movie. Slowly, she made her way to her homeroom, gliding her hand over lockers and kicking balls of paper across the floor.

She had about ten minutes to get to class before receiving a warning letter from her teacher. Of the ten minutes, six were spent staring at a wooden door. She visualized the bedlam that was unfolding in her class. A diminished smirk graced her as she heard a gallimaufry of shrills leak through the thin walls. A vague image formed in her head as she pushed the door open, and beyond it stood a picture-perfect scene of what had been imagined moments earlier. Aleia's smirk fully matured. Her eyes glanced over the classroom. A clique of girls sat on tabletops with almost half their uniform shirts unbuttoned; a group of boys was playing football, accompanied by a yell with every point; a couple was drawing matching tattoos in the corner, and a defeated teacher sat at her desk with one hand rubbing her temples and the other gripping a cup of coffee. Disregarding the pathetic image of the classroom, she calmly sat at her table and assimilated the setting around her. Pamphlets advertising the top ten universities decorated the walls around her, papers with tasks upon tasks were pinned to a bulletin board in front of her, and suddenly, the weight of the textbooks in her backpack felt a thousand tonnes heavier.

Aleia's heart began to race as she felt the weight of the future fall on her shoulders. She began discerning the pressure of the sheer *amount* of work that had to be finished in the upcoming years and every task that she hadn't done yet. A feeling of trepidation flooded through her body as she realized the implications of the future. Amidst this, her mind was hazed by anxiety. Her head felt light and dizzy, and something in her snapped. Her hands shook uncontrollably, leading her to shove them underneath the desk to ensure no one noticed her instability. *"You're so annoying. Why do you overact so much?"* She felt like there was a heavy weight falling on her chest, crushing her lungs and restraining her breath. The steady depletion of oxygen began taking away her conscience. Fear crept into her body like an unwanted guest as she placed her head on the table. Aleia managed to stay awake, her whole body lightly shaking with tears while clutching her hands close together under the furniture. She maintained a stoic expression, but the unsettling anxiety pushed her to keep still as droplets of salt delicately hit the desk over and over and over again.

AUGUST 24TH, 2017

She didn't know where she had gone wrong. The smile everyone always complimented her about, the musical laugh that everybody loved, or her positive attitude toward life ceased to exist. Her heart longed for the first time in four years as Aleia took her first steps into her junior year. *'I miss the old you. Where did you go? What happened to the joyful you? Why are you so sad? Shake it off, put on a smile. What's wrong with you? You're always in your room. No friends, no life. Nothing but a dying soul cooped up in her room. Why are you always hiding yourself away behind baggy clothes and layers of makeup?'* The thoughts and remarks never went away, only getting louder and louder with each passing day. She painted a pained smile and whispered to herself, "You're nothing. You're worthless. What are you if you can't even *fake* being happy?" It was almost like a mantra now, and she eventually realized no one was coming to break this cycle for her.

Like a signal from the Gods, the dark and stormy clouds finally released all the weight that they were carrying. The nimble raindrops hit the rough cobble pavement with incredible force, sounding like a drum kit gone rogue and accentuating the atmosphere of an upcoming storm. She curled her shaking hands into fists and stuffed them in her pockets. With a deep breath, she plugged her ears with the buds of her earphones, blasted her music at the highest volume and continued into the halls she dreaded to set foot on each day.

"Mrs Graham, Mrs Graham… God, where is her classroom?" she muttered with remote annoyance. The song ended. She continued to pass classes while hoping to locate the one she was scouring for. The song ended once more. The next one. The next. Over and over, a rhythm ended, and the next began. She discovered herself staring at a gap between two sets of lockers, wondering what it would feel like to be found in a locker yet again. Repressed memories gushed and took over her thoughts; the affliction she had held in her heart for so long barraged into her body like a long-standing dam wall crumbling, making her emotions crash into her at full force.

She smacked her face. "No. Stop it. Now is absolutely not the time," Aleia said to herself with alluded disappointment. She continued down the hallway and came across a plaque approximately ten feet north of where she was. It was a small rectangle neatly placed at the top of a door with a name boldly etched into it. Immediately, she had an urge to bang her head against the very appealing concrete wall before her. A feeling of familiarity met the somber teenager as she comprehended the room number. "*202, interesting,*" she voiced out loud. Through the waves of anxiety that flowed through her brain, she began reciting one word over and over in her most positive tone as she stood before the entrance to the classroom. "*Happy, happy, happy,*" she faked a smile.

One thing she learned from her parents and the exposure to witnessing her mom lead parades and marches was the power of first impressions. *"You're happy, all happy."* Who would ever want to interact with someone with an unhappy face and tears pooling in their eyes? She shook her head, attempting to knock off any signs that expressed her previous gloom, widened her grin, and slowly opened the door. A primarily empty classroom and the frowns of a small group of students ever so warmly greeted her. Aleia felt Mrs Graham's aura of fury ready to chew her out; however, the teacher's countenance immediately softened when she processed the identity of the girl awkwardly standing at the doorway.

"Aleia? It's quite unlikely to see you this late. Come in; I'll mark your presence," remarked the older, sweeter voice.

Aleia's face flushed in embarrassment. "Sorry, I was lost," she replied.

Looking up from the table, Mrs Graham stared her dead in the eye and raised an eyebrow. She didn't believe Aleia's excuse in the slightest, but decided to respect the student's privacy and kept her mouth shut. "Alright then, hurry up to your next class. If you didn't get your schedule, wait here with the rest of them," she said while vaguely pointing to the benches.

Her nose scrunched as she looked at the gang of guys lazing around the desk, chewing gum, and flexing their muscles. Aleia nervously tittered and responded, "No, thank you. I have my schedule, and um, I'll be going now." She sprinted down the crowding hallway and begrudgingly decided it was time for her to go to stupid algebra.

CHAPTER 2

SOCIETY? HAHA

The simplest atom
Evolves to contemplate its
Own evolution.

OCTOBER 18TH, 2017

"Social development? World peace? All we've learned because of society is to fear and betray one another. Every female, regardless of age, has to walk in *fear* as they pass by dark alleys or as they walk through empty roads at dusk. The cause isn't even imagination or a situation that has been thought of. The events that fuel the fear have occurred repeatedly, proving the decrepit state the world is in, and no human can justify otherwise. Why did the human mind become so corrupt, where half the populace is now identified as an object that can be played with? Do they not deserve bare homage, too? Sir, with all due respect, you speak of 'unity' and 'total peace,' yet there's someone out there getting raped for being confident. There's someone of color getting stopped and searched just for walking down the streets. Someone is getting denied a job purely because of disposition, gender, echelon, or appearance." She paused to take a deep breath, shakily exhaled, and continued. "There are so many minuscule problems but significant problems in the world, and we're all caught up in our vanity to realize. I hate the feeling of fear that boils at the pit of my chest when I leave the niche of my own home, and I despise the fact that no one addresses how iniquitous the situation is. I never understood why there were set rules determining who a person could be or what their future was purely based on gender or social class. Above all, it really amazes me how rapidly the world is developing in every aspect, yet the human mind is evolving backward with every passing moment."

She's been here for two months, and it's a fact that this teacher hates her, and she hates him. It's mutual hate. Aleia wouldn't have ever thought someone with such a low level of common knowledge could exist teaching social studies. It's the one subject where the utmost comprehension of past societal movements and current affairs is required, yet this guy managed to ignore both aspects. On top of that, he was mentally structured in a way that triggered a burning rage deep in her. The state of the world began building a true apprehension in her, knowing that sexual abuse was still a prominent issue, especially in public areas such as an office or schools. With every passing moment, the ideology her mom lives for makes more sense. As Aleia continues to view the world with lenses capturing the beauty and the ugly, the need for respect and importance increases. As she forms and expresses more emotions, people start insinuating that showing the bad alongside the good is forbidden.

As a woman, she has to maintain weight. Overeating is considered disgusting, and then immediately, no one can love you anymore. Eating too little will provide you with anorexia, but a socially acceptable body. She has to stay in line and maintain boundaries, but she can't fight back when someone crosses her limit because that would prove to be 'unladylike.' As a high-schooler, she must balance schoolwork, external work, a social life, her appearance to impress, and her grades. She needs to cope with the never-ending feeling of not being enough, the requirement to make people happy while being internally numb, the facade of joy every time someone is around, and the guilt for feeling tired or depressed. As a child, she just wanted to be understood and loved without pressurized barriers, forcing her to showcase positivity vividly. She's happy, though. In her eyes, what she goes through every day is worth it if she isn't a burden to her friends, family, or even someone she just met.

A tender, dramatic applause instantaneously brought her out of her mental tirade. She felt a wave of fatigue crash over her and realized her adrenaline was leaving her body. With a heavy sigh, she plopped onto the chair below her and, in confusion, saw a guy stand up from beside her. He continued to clap, and in a matter of seconds, all her other frustrated classmates followed suit. Aleia continued to stare at her initial supporter, noticing that his cheeks tinted pink when he realized he was being looked at. She vaguely remembered that his name was Aiden, the shy but funny guy who never really spoke up in class. They worked together on a Shakespearean English project a while ago and have never interacted since.

The steady, sharp sound that rhythmically resounded through the room began triggering some form of abhorrence in the professor. At this point, he practically had wisps of steam blowing out of his ears, his face being bright pink. His tomato-red nose was scrunched up in a manner that resembled a pig's snout, causing the blinding image of Peppa Pig to flash before her eyes. Then, it crumbled. All the defenses she put up to maintain discipline and proper social behavior in class went down the drain. She let out a snort, followed by a series of giggles. She laughed about all the stress she had, the appearance of her gnome-looking teacher, and the fact that she snorted in front of fifty people. She just laughed until one hand clutched her stomach, the other covering the bottom half of her face, and tears threatened to overflow her eyes. Aleia barely noticed the ascending rage from her teacher and the eyes that were filled with endearment looking at her.

"STOP." The professor was taking deep (loud) breaths, and his eyebrows furrowed in an attempt to look furious. "Ms. Ledger, get out of the room right now." At this point, Aleia was really trying to tame her laughter. The whole situation seemed so whimsical, but her heart went still when she realized the consequences she would face if she didn't comply now. She gently pushed the table forward, making room to get up. As she was in the process of getting up, Aleia was softly pushed back into her seat. She sharply snapped her head up with confusion.

"What–?" she started.

"No," his reply came. Aleia's enhanced confusion must have been distinctly visible on her face because Aiden glanced at her and smiled in amusement. He continued, "She hasn't done anything wrong, and it would prove every one of her points if you just kicked her out."

The professor retaliated by mentioning inappropriate classroom behavior and how some societal norms and stigmas exist for reasons we were too young to understand.

His sheer condescension clearly triggered a significant fraction of the class as they began rising too. A few claps and soft cheers echoed through the room, and one kid shouted, "Viva la resistance."

Aiden triumphantly smirked and calmly said, "We'll be leaving, then."

Aleia's eyes widened as she witnessed what was happening. Her mouth slightly hung agape with surprise when she saw each student make their way out of the room, ignoring the teacher's curses and threats to send them to a higher authority. Who would have thought she could inspire people? A wave of pride, followed by gratitude, washed over her. She couldn't bring herself to get up from her seat and follow her classmates as they beelined for the door.

As Aleia sat there thinking about her crazy outburst to one stupid comment about how we as a human race achieved world peace, the fact that someone stood up to her, and the idea that she might have made a genuine friend caused one thought to repeat over and over in her mind: "Damn, I started a revolution."

CHAPTER 3

HAPPY BIRTHDAY?

A caterpillar,

This deep in fall,

Still not a butterfly.

By Matsuo Basho

NOVEMBER 21ST, 2017

'Why do we celebrate birthdays?' she wondered. 'What was the point?'

It was a celebration that proved an individual had grown one year closer to death and achieved almost nothing. What was it, if not a symbol that merely represented another year closer to death?

It was 4:30, and there was half an hour left until her birthday party officially started. She had called most of her class and some close neighbors. Though she knew they liked her because of her upbeat personality, Aleia wasn't sure if enough people would attend to be able to call it a party. The lack of people was a frequent occurrence, and it became more amusing than mean, so she cracked a facetious joke and moved on. However, her parents were tremendously more optimistic than her and made the occasion the best it could be.

She sat on one of the beautiful cream tables littering her lawn. The curved bottom of the tablecloth was embroidered with cute lavender flowers and their leaves, circling the entire circumference. At the center of the table was a slim cylindrical glass vase that contained those very flowers, adding a certain depth, life, and fragrance to the scene. Fairy lights lit up above her head. Most of them were concentrated around the stage, which held her 'throne' (which she was supposed to be grandiloquently residing on). Aleia stared at her long, pale fingers that were currently twirling a small piece of fabric from the skirt of her dress. Her nails were painted off-white, with small hand-painted butterflies and gems glittering the length. Her hands had so many minimalistic rings and bracelets that she looked like a princess from the fanciest kingdom around. She contentedly smiled as her fingertips grazed the topmost layer of rough chiffon on her dress. Her legs were completely covered with a hundred layers of varying types of cloth to create the perfect ball gown. The color was subtle but could have been seen and identified from hundreds of meters away. The hue was a blend of lilac and periwinkle, beautifully adorned with silver butterflies and pearls.

The aroma of hot, freshly unpacked food wafted through the air, generating a familiar sound that typically emerged an hour before lunchtime in school. She was so hungry. She was so unbelievably hungry, and she didn't even know why. She yearned for a burrito; that's all she had ever wanted. It felt like a piece of her heart died when her favorite burrito place burned down right in front of her eyes. Aleia kept staring at her hands with a disposition that was presumably concerning as her dad startled her back to the present.

"Are you okay?" he questioned.

"I'm so hungry," she frowned.

Her father laughed at her bluntness and helped her get up. "Come on, someone's at the door."

Aleia's eyebrows shot up to her hairline. "Well, *that*," she paused, is surprising."

As Aleia made her way through her home, she realized how well-decorated it actually was. Because she spent the greater part of the day at her birthday breakfast, getting ready, and then in her backyard, she hadn't discovered the streamers that adorned the walls. She turned the corner and saw her mom talking to someone by the doorway, practically jumping with excitement. It seemed they had noticed Aleia's prominent presence because her mom shifted back and turned to reveal a set of auburn eyes staring at her. Her head cocked to the side in confusion.

"Aiden?"

He sheepishly grinned and said, "The one and only."

A million thoughts raced through her mind. It was shocking to see that he came at all, and even more so that he was the first one there. It did warm her heart, though. He was one of the only people who had seen her talk without a mask to hide her feelings.

She smiled softly and responded, "Alright, follow me out back. The party's on the lawn, but be warned, you're the first one here, so there's a lot of seats to choose from."

The raven-haired boy pursued the brunette in soft silence until their destination stood before them. Nothing was perfect, but Aleia would call it reasonably close as she viewed the area once more from a distance.

"You should enjoy yourself. No one's going to be here for a while anyway. If you get hungry, feel free to help yourself to a snack and a drink, and I will be, uh," Aleia paused before continuing, "just walking around, I suppose."

"I hope I'm not crossing any boundaries, but I just wanted to say you looked pulchritudinous." Aiden corrected himself upon seeing the dazed look on the birthday girl's face. "You look beautiful, I meant."

A deep red dusting covered Aleia's cheeks. He continued the conversation by making her sit on one of the wooden chairs, telling her they should use this time to get to know each other, and promptly left to bring some refreshments. With every moment that passed, Aleia's anticipation and anxiety increased. It had been so long since she partook in legitimate, friendly chatter that didn't involve faking a smile and only saying 'hello.' *He* had approached her, which lifted the judging gaze of a thousand eyes from every word she said.

In the distance, Aleia saw a blurry blob walking in her direction. She immediately realized how bad her sight had become. A moment later, Aiden was looming above her, carrying a giant bucket of fries and two smoothies.

"How about we play a game? We could do two truths and one lie, and you'd have to guess the fib," asked the boy.

Aleia smiled, "I love that idea."

The two teenagers began talking, exchanging their hobbies, likes, dislikes, what they do in their free time, and any other possible information that was slowly blooming into a hopeful friendship. She didn't have to force affability or happiness as she talked. Sure, she wasn't as 'joyful' as she was in class, but naturally, she was almost there. People began pouring into the lawn as time passed. In between, she had to leave her light-hearted talk to go and meet with her other guests, but the girl was back in no longer than five minutes.

"How come we never talked before? You seem like such a great friend. You're always so cheerful and positive in class, and truly, that's so alluring. It's cool to see how much calmer you are in person," came Aiden's voice as she retook her seat.

Not again. It felt like an arrow shot through her heart. Aiden probably just found her amiable from afar, and once they collided, his expectations didn't meet reality. Her emotion right now wasn't enough to fulfill the assumptions. She knew she was being irrational.

The lack of response prompted him to speak again, "Hey, you okay? You seem a bit sad."

"I'm okay, yes," she wistfully responded.

"Cheer up! You should have the best time. It's your birthday, after all."

That tied the knot in her throat. It was a physical manifestation of the emotional turmoil she was experiencing. She could feel the familiar tingling in her nose and burn in her eyes. The lush grass, tablecloth, food, Aiden, and the world around her blurred as a teardrop threatened to escape.

"Excuse me," she whispered.

Then Aleia ran. She ran with the wind, acting like her wings, maneuvering through tables and chairs until she found the first room and charged inside.

The tears held by her eyes left their captor as the bathroom door slammed behind her. She glared at her reflection in the mirror with execration. Her eyes were turning bloodshot, her nose was red with tears, and her chest hurt. It felt like an army of evil butterflies stormed her gut. Her head felt like it weighed nothing, while her entire body weight was dragging her down. She felt like she had the pressure of the world on her shoulders, and she didn't know why. She started making one friend, maybe someone who would genuinely like her for her, but it was her fault a small prick could break her facade. She was so close, but so far. "*He spared himself, honestly. The last thing someone would want is to be a friend of mine,*" she thought.

"Nothing you can do is ever going to be right," she sobbed to the empty room that surrounded her. She was overwhelmed. She was falling behind in every aspect, and at the same time, she was falling down. Aleia was dropping off of a cliff to the bottom of hell. Her head bowed down with forfeit.

"Your parents worked so hard to get you to where you are. You were born with a silver spoon, yet you're doing nothing but exploiting it. You don't deserve this luxury. You don't deserve this love," she whispered.

"How many people roaming in your lawn don't know what a monster you are?"

She was trembling against the wooden door, with both hands clenching the picture-perfect dress. "You ruin everything," she said.

Her head shot up to the mirror; she stared at her eyes. She looked maniacal. "I HATE YOU!" she screamed. The three words were repeated over and over again, and each repetition had a lower amplitude than the last.

She slowly slid down till the bottom of her back touched the ground. Aleia miserably stared at the gorgeous, gold-ornated cupboards before her. She thought about how pretty the details were against the white wood. She recalled how excited her mom was when they got them installed. Aleia knew she was drowning. All she wanted was the rope that would save her. She knew that rope would burn her palms if she were to be pulled out, but she didn't really care. She needed that escape, regardless of the damage it did. But she didn't have that rope. She didn't have any means of escape. She felt stranded in the middle of the ocean, doing nothing but float as water filled her lungs. All she could do in the present was suffer.

A dry laugh resonated through the room. "You have no identity. You've built so many walls to block out any 'wrong' emotions that could be displayed in public; no one knows your pain anymore. You learned to appeal to everyone's expectations of behavior and sentiment; you lost yourself. Who created this social stigma?"

A tearless sob escaped her. "I just wanted to tell people how I feel. But that would be selfish and attention-seeking, wouldn't it?"

Aleia used her knuckles to wipe away the wetness on her cheeks. "You have no genuine relationships. Your parents think you have no pressure and that you're doing okay. They care for you so much, but you repay them with nothing. All the friends you've made don't talk to you unless you approach first. You had one shot of making a true friend, but you blew that. Maybe it's because you have no personality."

Her eyes, nose, and face were dry now, she decided. Carefully, she got up in her 4-inch silver, butterfly-adorned heels, ensuring she did not trip on her dress. Aleia ambled toward the sink to wash her hands. She inspected her hair and makeup and determined that the only significant casualty was some lost blush. Thank the gods for waterproof mascara.

"Seventeen years, and you achieved nothing. Happy birthday."

***

It was almost 6 PM now. She walked through the lawn, attempting to enjoy the music and atmosphere, praying that no one noticed her absence. She hoped to calm down with the live band and food before encountering anyone who would tick her off again. Weirdly, no more than 4 people were in her vicinity, excluding her. It can't be that hard to forget the birthday girl, can it? Like a sign of irony from the heavens, she was immediately contradicted.

"Hey! Where were you? We've been looking for you for so long," came Aiden's voice from behind her. His speed eventually caught up with hers, and she could see the worry glistening in his eyes. Her heart felt warm to see someone show concern for her.

'He's just being a decent human; he doesn't care for you.'

"You had me worried. You disappeared for so long, in between conversations too. I was kinda worried I did something wrong."

She stared at him, appalled. "This is the first time we genuinely talked," she commented.

He smiled the purest smile she had ever seen. "I grow fond of people easily."

She couldn't explain it. Aleia was so oddly drawn to this boy. Maybe it was the twinkle in his eyes, how his thick, black hair was like a mop on his head, the silly smile he almost always had painted on, the blush on his cheeks that subtly complemented his slightly tan skin, or how easy it was to be around him. She didn't feel that pressure to be happy around him. She knew she wasn't going to be judged.

Noticing her silence, Aiden followed with, "Alright! No time to lose. Follow me."

He took hold of her wrist and pulled her through the glass doors, zigzagging through the corridors of her home, and finally paused when they stood before a pitch-black room.

She knew what was about to happen, but that didn't mean it wasn't exciting. Bright fluorescent lights illuminated above her; warm yellow fairy lights were generously placed all over the living room, and she could see paper mâché butterflies hung from the ceiling. That's all she comprehended before a united chorus of birthday greetings overtook her, and two 'POP!' sounds erupted, dispersing multicolored paper hearts through the air. Her parents held an elegant circular white cake adorned with pearls, miniature pink buttercream roses gently placed on the thick detailing around the borders, and a greeting written with fondant in the middle. Candles shaped like the number '17' were lit under one of the curves of the heart. Gradually, the lights dimmed, and she was handed a slim, translucent plastic knife.

Aleia stepped closer to the cake, blowing out her candles and cutting the cake as her guests started singing 'Happy Birthday'. She basked in the presence of happiness from her parents, enjoying the pictures taken as everyone gathered around her.

As the party began winding down, Aleia's mom looked at the birthday girl with so much love and affection. She delicately kissed her daughter on the cheek and embraced her for a hug.

In a hushed tone, she whispered, "Happy birthday, sweetie."

CHAPTER 4

THE SPIRIT OF MIRACLES

Love between us is

speech and breath. Loving you is,

A long river running.

By Sonia Sanchez

DECEMBER 24TH, 2017

Soft, angelic snow fell from the skies, mixing with the clouds' carefully crystallized and crafted snowflakes. It turned the tops of pine and fir trees white, and the excess painted the tar roads like vanilla frosting. Every time a harsh wind blew, Aleia could feel the ice crystals press against her face and neck, lightly dampening it. No matter how hard she tried, the brisk chill of Christmas broke through her clothing. It was so cold that the poor girl was completely decked out, yet she still shivered. She had three layers of tops, beginning from a simple peach camisole underneath a white collared shirt, and the significant keeper of warmth was a sea-green sweater. On the other half, Aleia styled herself with fleece tights, a black, pleated mini-skirt, and shin-length black boots. A few strands of hair framed her face, and the rest was held back with a big, deep green bow. She loved dressing up, even if it wasn't a big event, and that was pretty evident based on how she dressed for her mom's work event. Christmas Eve parties were among the most celebrated of the year, and her mom's activist group hosts the best one each time.

Until the previous Christmas, she wasn't allowed at the party because she was considered 'too young', but when she discovered the event's excellence, nothing in the world prevented her from going.

This morning, her mom told her she could invite one of her friends, gave her a mischievous wink, and left Aleia in shock. So, here she was, walking by Aiden as they made their way to the venue. They had been talking continuously for around a month. They often visited each other, played video games together, and ended up having meals together, so it was no surprise that they became this close. It was almost half past 6 in the evening, and the festivity began at 8 PM, giving them two hours to kill (obviously, they can't be the first ones there). They started early, so they decided to walk, and since the hotel wasn't far, they also decided to take a more scenic route.

They entered the central metropolitan area of their city, almost wishing they had sunglasses because of the intensity of the light. Shrubbery lined the pavements, adding a pop of green to the dull mixture of cement, brick, and tar. Uniquely shaped LED bulbs littered the branches of pine trees. The streets were adorned with stars, hearts, circles, and teardrops. Colorful lights hung in intricate patterns on every building, street lamp, and windowsill. The commercial establishments were lined with ginormous flat screens displaying advertisements for various products. Some had images of Christmas trees; others played bulletins for luxury-branded clothing and shoe stores. Giant Christmas trees, covered with glittering ornaments and twinkling lights, towered over the bustling crowds. Large ornaments and wreaths of holly and pine were hung on shopfronts and residential doors. The air was filled with the scent of pine needles and cinnamon as vendors sold freshly baked gingerbread and roasted chestnuts on every corner. The warm aroma of hot chocolate wafted from cafes, tempting passersby with its rich sweetness. The sweet fragrance of candied fruits found its way to Aleia's nose, enticing her to stop her journey and indulge in overly priced foods. As clumps of people walked by, she could see little puffs of snow lift off the soles of people's shoes. She felt Aiden's soft mittens graze against her palm, gently reminding her he was with her in the mob of people. The sound of Christmas carols echoed through the streets, making it a magical sight to behold.

To kill time, they enjoyed window shopping at fancy stores and visiting small stalls for all sorts of merchandise and foods. Eventually, they found themselves in a heightened corner, each holding cups of hot cocoa that kept their hands warm. As they consumed the beverage, the hot cocoa turned into more than just a drink; it was a moment of camaraderie. Like tiny clouds, miniature marshmallows were afloat on the rich, velvety drink. With every sip, the warmth spread through them, from the cocoa's heat, the laughter they exchanged, and their gleeful, childlike happiness. It became a moment frozen in time, where the cold outside was met with the warmth of friendship.

The two teenagers slowly made their way to the hotel, sighing in relief when they saw the structure. The warm yellow lights in the lobby seemed so welcoming in contrast to the harsh chill outside. Cute cardboard cutouts of Christmas trees were hung from the ceiling, complementing a miniature gingerbread house built in the hallway. It was decorated with comically large candy canes, a dusting of fake snow, and plastic gumdrops and candies.

They lazed around in the lobby for a while, watching the hotel's advertisements on a TV while snacking on free cookie samples (Aiden stuffed a few in his suit's pocket). When the delicately crafted wooden grandfather clock beside the help desk struck 8:30, Aleia resolved it was time to go and join the event they had come for. They briefly interrogated the hotel staff about where the event was happening and navigated their way through the building to the ballroom (1).

Aleia was immediately and cheerfully greeted by her mom, who was already so excited about 'how well everything was going'. After bombarding Aleia with questions about her well-being, she began introducing her daughter to others who were helping her reform sexist laws. One stark trait she found was the shared passion for their cause and their 'all-or-nothing' attitude. Though it had only been ten minutes, she was inspired. Because of this, Aleia decided to pursue this route of conversation, dragging Aiden with her. She ended up learning a lot about their movements, how they built cases, and their primary goal. Aleia was fascinated by how such a small group of people could make the world a better place. She loved how it promoted fairness to all, consequently developing the world in ways industries can't.

Shortly, a grand feast commenced. Various foods were spread on a long, rectangular table ranging from exotic and imported to warm and home-cooked. Baked potatoes, beans, salads, cold seafood, roast chicken breast, plum pudding, apple pies, and custard all took their positions. Gold-plated cutlery, tissue paper swans, and beautifully decorated porcelain plates were laid out at each seat, creating a set that resembled 'The Last Supper'. Bottles of old, expensive French wine were placed periodically along the table, and flasks of whiskey and scotch accompanied each one (for those who wanted something more potent).

After the extravagant feast, she went to the bar to get a soda, where she heard her name being called. A young woman, maybe in her early twenties, bellowed 'HEY!' in a deep voice, indicating that she was coming. She had a lean, toned frame, which was evident by the corsetted tank top she high-key rocked. Tattoos of various sizes, colors, and shapes formed a sleeve around her arms, making most of her bare, pale skin disappear. Five piercings lined each ear, plainly visible as her rich black hair was shabbily tucked behind her ears. She concluded that the lady had dived deep into the 'badass' look but was still undecided about her personality. The holes in her ears were filled with glimmering stars and ornamental designs, alluding to her being sweet and warm rather than scary. The lady stopped walking when she was a few feet away from Aleia. With a beaming grin, she stuck her hand straight out, made a 'grabby' motion, and introduced herself with a slight slur in her voice.

"Hi! I'm Nova."

Aleia eyed her up and down and then understood: Nova was tipsy. Aiden, who was just out of earshot, began gaining intrigue in the unfolding image and joined them.

"Hi, I'm Aleia– Catherine's daughter," came Aleia's reply.

"DUDE! MRS. LEDGER IS SO COOL!"

The teenagers' eyebrows shot up. They agreed, but the statement itself was so out of the blue.

"How so?"

Nova clapped her hands and exclaimed delightfully, "OH MY GOD, OKAY, YOU *NEED* TO KNOW THIS STORY." She clumsily took a seat on a bar stool, and the other two kids followed suit.

She continued, "So, a few years ago, there was a huge chain of paper companies, and for Christmas, they had to give *all* their employees bonuses–." She paused.

"Hey," she called to the bartender, "could I get another glass of champagne, please?"

It almost seemed like she lost her train of thought because Nova didn't continue speaking after the request. Aleia was about to ask her to continue, but the pitch of the words that came out of her mouth was much deeper than her voice. Then she realized that they weren't her words. Aiden prompted Nova to continue, and their sync in feelings made her feel fuzzy inside.

"What–? Oh! Right. So their shitty boss gave the guys ginormous sums of money and gave the women pennies and nickels." Nova placed her palms on Aleia's shoulders and shook her vigorously while yelling, "PENNIES AND NICKELS, ALEIA!"

She continued, "The worst part was his justification, which claimed a 'substantial difference in work quality.'

Obviously, the women sued the guy, and your mom worked so much overtime simply by combing through files and laws to prove to the judge that the women deserved equal bonuses, AND THE BEST PART IS THAT SHE DID IT. You should be so proud of her."

Aleia saw her mom laughing with her friends in the distance, emanating pure, unfiltered joy. She smiled, "I really am."

Nova took a big gulp of her remaining alcohol and said, "Alright, that's it for me. You kiddos have fun drinking your mocktails and orange juice," with a dazed expression. Then, she left.

"I'm so happy they got what they deserved," came Aiden's voice from beside her.

A light blush tinted her face. "Same," she agreed, thinking about her social studies teacher in school.

"It honestly sucks how people like that still exist. It's no lie that women have so much more on their plate, and being treated like that is so disheartening. Mrs. Ledger did so much good for the company. I feel like becoming a lawyer right now. Wait, no, I feel like punching that stupid—" his digression was cut off by an embarrassed voice behind them.

A waiter balancing a dozen empty glasses on a tray awkwardly asked him to step aside because he was blocking the way. Aiden turned red. His face morphed into a beetroot, his eyes widened in horror and his hand went flying to cover his mouth.

"I-Oh my god, I am so sorry. I am very sorry, sir. I'm moving right now."

Aiden spoke with a muffle, but what came out wasn't his usual tone. He emitted a squeaky, high-pitched voice, and Aleia could not get enough of it. She clutched her stomach and leaned against the table, shaking with laughter. Her face was flushed, with her trying to keep her giggles in check, and she was turning breathless with the lack of circulation. The situation was ridiculously amusing; combining that with Aiden's embarrassment and many voice cracks turns it into a free laughter therapy session.

Between fits of laughter, Aleia wheezed, "Come on, let's find a place to sit."

After a brief expedition, they found a teeny royal blue sofa tucked away behind a cluster of tables. It was shoved against a wall, and there was a kids' desk in front of it, so they had to shimmy their knees into the gap under the table maladroitly (thankfully, they fit; they were both short enough). She sat first, cozying up in the corner. He slowly came in after, and due to the tight space, his knee gently brushed against hers. She didn't know why, but his touch spawned a flight of butterflies in her stomach. Aleia fully expected him to move away after he settled, but he didn't. He just stared at the small point of contact with the goofiest smile on his face and sniffed. She thought he began crying, but he sheepishly whispered, "I think I have a cold."

Then he started laughing. It was a situation she found genuinely magical. They were minutes away from Christmas; they were together, and all she could look at and feel was the warmth radiating off him. She had never felt so whole before.

Aiden was a person who never faked his identity with anyone. He was crystal clear about who he was and what he wanted to say.

On the other hand, she hid everything from everyone. No one knew how she felt, what she was feeling, or what could be done to help, except him. They were opposites, but the fact that someone as open as him accepted her true self completely seemed impossible. He was so special. Call her drunk on Christmas miracles, but it felt like they were made for each other.

The clock rang. It chimed so readily, signaling a new day. It continued to ring, but all the noise was blurred out.

Aleia simply stared at him with tears welling in her eyes. Her body was filled with a sense of *home*.

Aiden's laughter slowly died down. He leaned his head against the wall and turned toward the blushing girl.

The clock continued to ring.

Familiar explosions erupted outside, splashing the midnight sky with scintillating colors.

Loud booms rang in her ears as Aiden took her hand and held it with two of his own. His eyes were twinkling, and he looked ethereal. His nose and cheeks were flushed with laughter; his lips were full of color, and his mop of thick black hair was disheveled. His almond-shaped eyes were almost shut close with the size of his smile.

He whispered, "Merry Christmas, Aleia."

CHAPTER 5

THE BEGINNING OF THE END

"Shall we die?"
You whispered to me,
At the night of firefly.

By Suzuki Masajo

JANUARY 7TH, 2018

Aleia couldn't remember a time when she was happier. Everything she really wanted to accomplish had been fulfilled. She found a friend she could be true to herself with, and in that friend, she found someone she could love. Also, Aleia made it to her seventeenth birthday, so all her goals were marked as checked. She was splayed on her fluffy white bed, staring at the cream ceiling above her. The fan spun slowly, and she could faintly hear birdsong through her glass windows. She loved how comfortable her bed was: shoved to the corner of her room, making it seem like the walls shielded her, and filled to the brim with pillows and comforters.

Beams of morning light were cast into the room, illuminating a small pastel pink rug. A stack of folded clothes was lying on a white wooden stool that stood in front of her cupboard. It was a perfectly normal day, except for the fact that she theoretically died today. A couple of months ago, she marked a date on her calendar that she thought would be perfect. She would've lived a long enough life by then; it was after every significant celebration and the beginning of a new year. This date was also the first Sunday of the year, meaning she wouldn't have to go through any Monday blues. However, her past self didn't know that Aleia had found something to live for and look forward to.

She groggily propped herself up on the bed to view the paper calendar hung on the wall in front of her, next to her vanity table. There it was - a bold red ring around January 7th with two lines going through it. With the felicity that currently filled her soul, the markings looked plain wrong. Aleia left her position on the bed and let her soles relish in the cold touch of the marble. She walked over to the large flap of dates while stepping over her unfinished homework and picking up a black CD marker on the way. She shabbily scratched out the circles and lines and replaced them with a book, symbolizing the half-down worksheets spread across the floor.

That reminded her she should probably get back to it. She plopped down on the floor in her pajamas and decided to keep working until her stomach started eating itself, or someone special called her.

JANUARY 11TH, 2018

She remembered what happens when she gets too close to someone. Aleia remembered her frustration while analyzing every little thing she could have done wrong when their mood slightly shifted. She knew she wasn't the perfect person to talk to. Aleia knew she wasn't the happiest and that she couldn't make other people the happiest they could be either. But was it wrong for her to assume she made him happy?

It was just another school day. Once more, she had to sit through hours of classes, waiting for lunch, then slog through another two hours while waiting for the home bell to ring. Her last class was AP Biology, and as enjoyable as it was, she was more than relieved to hear the 'trrring' that signaled the end of the school day. Aleia had had enough of faking her interest in classmate conversations and fatigue. The girl raced out of the building in hopes of spotting only one person.

'Am I being too clingy?'
Aiden was hanging out under a large oak tree, talking and laughing with his friends. Their laughter echoed in the air, blending harmoniously with the gentle rustling of leaves in the breeze. His eyes were bright, conveying a genuine happiness that warmed her from within. Aleia's gaze softened as she observed Aiden's animated gestures, each movement accompanied by an infectious energy. All else flew out of her mind at that point, and she began sprinting in that direction. Once she neared them, she slowed down. Her heavy breaths tolled loudly in her ears, and once she calmed down, only his twinkling laughter was heard. She awkwardly stood a distance away from them, far enough not to intrude, and she prayed she was close enough for her only friend to notice her presence.

While another student was engaging in conversation, Aiden briefly turned in Aleia's direction, stared at his friend again, widened his eyes when he realized Aleia was there, and locked eyes with her. The sparkle in his eyes got a thousand times brighter, a slight grin graced his lips, and his chuckles died down. The joyous boy excused himself and walked toward her until they were a few feet apart.

His face was glowing with happiness; a small dimple took its place high on one cheek, and a wide, gaiety grin flattered the rest of his features.

He looked beautiful. Aleia couldn't get herself to look away. That also meant she looked like a strawberry, given her flustered appearance. The heat spreading in her face felt so embarrassing that she tucked it away into her palms and bowed her head down. She wondered if he was interested in hanging out in a nearby cafe and immediately became determined to ask him. When she looked up again (she knew she was still a little pink), his expression had changed. He looked sadder.

His hearty laughs were substituted with a mellow frown. His face relaxed to portray a more fatigued emotion, and the rapture in his eyes was quickly replaced with confusion and concern. She couldn't bring herself to speak.

"Are you okay?" Aiden asked quietly.

Aleia was getting increasingly panicked about his immediate shift in mood since he left his friends.

No reply came. Aiden tenderly tapped her shoulder. "Aleia?" he prompted again.

She was being irrational, but the fear of rejection gnawed at her heart. Doubt clouded her mind like a dense fog, and she questioned whether Aiden truly wanted to talk to her at all. She felt a pang of insecurity gnawing at her confidence. *'Is he weirded out?'*

Her throat tightened. Aiden was so happy earlier, so full of laughter; did she make him sad? He probably didn't want to talk to her, which made sense. *'Why do I ruin everything?'* she thought. Her chest clenched with pain.

"Uh, yeah. I just wanted to say bye. Sorry," Aleia murmured.

His eyebrows creased. Aleia wrung her hands together and walked out of school, giving her tear ducts a workout by trying her best to keep the salty liquid in. She vaguely heard Aiden calling for her from a distance, but she didn't look back or respond, in worry of making his mood worse.

They didn't talk much that day.

JANUARY 13TH, 2018

It happened again.

Aleia was 'friends' with many people from school, primarily because she was considered the best idealistic friend. Her vanity stated that she was always cheerful, had no drama tied to her, was bright and was happy to help with any situation. This meant that she had a considerable number of mutual friends with Aiden.

They were out celebrating one of her classmates' birthdays. It was the go-to option when planning birthday parties - tiring out at an arcade, then raiding a restaurant. It was a considerably large group, with around fifteen people. Aleia was aware that her time with Aiden would be less, but she didn't know how downhill their little time together would go.

Societal norms segregated the activities in the arcade into 'boys and girls'. The guys commended each other with immense enthusiasm every time they got something from a claw machine, and the girls just went into rage mode on the basketball minigame. The two friends had never managed to cross paths as the party maintained this divide.

They did at the restaurant, however. The birthday girl booked a private sector for their meal, so after the ceremonial cake-cutting, people were too hungry to participate in any activities. Aiden talked to the birthday girl, exchanging jokes and making the others laugh. He looked so free.

Aleia took a seat at the table and rested her head against the wall. She was tired, and it seemed like she had jinxed herself because she hadn't felt mentally well the past few days. The familiar desperation to save herself became constant again, and it felt like she was losing everything. She had no idea how the situation had changed so drastically.

"Hi."

Aleia turned to the direction of the voice. She was met with Aiden's face, full of childlike innocence and joy. A smile automatically appeared. She replied softly, "Hi."

She was laconic as they conversed, and she noticed Aiden's evident, rapid degradation of mood.

Aleia cut him off, "What did I do wrong?"

His eyes widened with surprise. "Nothing, really. It's just that you don't seem as happy anymore."

She turned back to face the ceiling. "I see," she said with a solemn smile. Aiden frowned, wished her farewell, slowly got up and left.

Three words resounded in her head, *'You lost everything.'*

JANUARY 20ᵀᴴ, 2018

That was the day it all went to hell. That was the day she was going to die.

It was a serene morning with baby blue skies and long tendrils of white clouds gracing it. She knew what would occur over the day and genuinely never felt freer. The sweet aroma of breakfast lured her out of her room, where she met her dad making differently shaped pancakes. As she sat at the table, she complimented the food and asked him, "Do you guys want to watch a movie later?" As an afterthought, she added, "I'm up for anything."

Her father raised an eyebrow as he put a stack of pancakes on her plate. "Sadly, no. I'm planning a cute lunch date with your mom because she's been sending me obvious hints, and I get the feeling that she wants to go on one," he replied.

"You'll be okay at home, though, right?" her father asked warily, and to that, she gave him her assurance.

After a bit, he spoke again, "You seem happy again. We were worried about how dull you were these past few days."

Aleia's soft smile turned upside down. "Don't fret over me. From today, I'll be completely off your shoulders. You guys, have fun, okay? I'll be in my room."

✳✳✳

The last of the walls meant to suppress her emotions tumbled down. She was vulnerable and exposed and had no energy to hide anything. The window of time left while she was home alone was getting significantly narrower.

Aleia finished composing two perfect notes; one of them was hand-written and left on her bed in a tiny pink envelope. The other was a text to Aiden, alluding that she was leaving the world. She stared at the screen, wondering if she should hit send.

'*We're all dying anyway, and once I do, I'll decompose into pretty flowers. If I'm lucky, the bees would choose me for pollination, and maybe the kids you have with a perfect girl would drink tea with the honey they make.*'

"You're pathetic,"

"You deserve nothing," she opened the liquor cupboard and picked up a flask. Her expertise in alcohol classification was limited, so she just hoped she got the strongest one.

Her mind was still, simply moving along with the orchestra of her limbs. Her situation was an act that played through her head thousands of times. She imagined these exact movements, always wishing to execute them, but she kept holding on to an invisible hope that something would get better. But now? *Now*, she was done. She held on for a week, as tight as she could, simply praying that the pain would go away. But it was so tiring. She had nothing left to live for. Nothing made her want to get out of bed in the morning. Aleia had enough. She had no identity; it disappeared under the mound of lies, her so-called relationships. With shaking hands, she rummaged through the medication cabinet, praying her mom didn't throw out the sleeping pills. During the summer before eleventh-grade, she had ridiculously severe insomnia. Every night, her mind was her enemy. She was so overwhelmed by her thoughts that she couldn't move. In the dead of night, her heart continued to ache while the fear of awakening her parents silenced her cries. When the doctor suggested sleep and anxiety medication, she agreed. The pain of the consequences wasn't as bad as what she felt at midnight. Over time, a pill a night became 2. Nausea, migraines, dizziness, and hallucinations became normal. She was completely fine with that; in fact, she was happy if it meant she could experience those few hours of numbness. When her parents found out, their shock was greater than anything she'd seen before. Aleia was no longer allowed to open that cabinet, and the cycle began once more the following summer.

'I bet they would be even more shocked now,' she bitterly thought.

At the very back, she saw the familiar cylindrical container. With shaking hands and blurry eyes, she took it and tried to decipher the worn-out label to confirm the drug.

She grabbed the bottle, headed to her room and locked herself in.

She took a massive swig of whatever was in the flask, involuntarily shaking her head from the jolt of bitterness. Deciding it was a good time, she sent the message to Aiden, hoping he wouldn't open it for a while. The loud voices in her head immediately were muffled, as though they were forcefully stuffed into a box. Aleia then pulled the cap off the capsule container and swallowed one. To wash it down, she took in more of the liquid. The seventeen-year-old continued to alternate the drugs until she knew she hit the vertex. It felt like she was blinking exceptionally slowly and that her body no longer considered her brain its ruler. Colors became less saturated, and her mouth turned to rubber. Her ears rang with great intensity, throwing her off even more in her disoriented state. Everything seemed distant - the flicker of her fluorescent lights, the laughter of children playing football from the streets, the shuffling feet outside her door - blurring into a soft, incomprehensible haze as her mind struggled to keep up with the flurry of emotion within her. She knew that her grasp on her consciousness was weakening, and in a flurry of movement, she tried finding a support that would break her fall. She burned to the touch, but the shivering fits never seemed to end. Her limbs felt like they weren't there, and her skin no longer processed the tears that rolled down her cheeks.

She couldn't see; she couldn't feel, and then she collapsed.

Aleia saw herself through a hazed vision as if she was standing behind a foggy screen. She was floating. No, she was falling. She was riding the winds thousands of feet above the vicious ocean she was bound to collide with. The girl felt the undisturbed atmosphere surround her, making her feel the cool grip of death embracing her. Her head didn't feel like it was being held down by a thousand-tonne brick anymore. Her hair was freely flying as her clothes slowly began rending apart with the pressure. She curled her fingers around the clouds that were present in all directions, blocking any vision she had for escape. She tried holding onto the pressure of the atmosphere. It was so thick she felt like her body weight was the only thing that let her cut through it. Yet, she couldn't grasp anything. The air slipped through the gaps of her tightly curled fist. Aleia could see that she began panicking. The expression of pleasure turned into one of fear. She wanted to escape but knew it was too late. She was already too far down. She closed her eyes. Aleia tried familiarizing herself with the environment. Gradually, she found the groove of ecstasy—a bitter smile formed on her face.

Two hundred meters from the water.

She felt her arms flail around her as her shoulder joints dislocated. She knew it was only the beginning of her freedom. She knew that this pain was worth the pleasure.

A hundred meters from the water.

The thought of pure escape obscured her mind. Her heart filled with hope and anticipation for what awaited her. She knew she had nothing left to give. Nothing made her feel the way she felt at that moment. Nothing had made her heart feel this light, as if it was made of nothing. The pressure was comforting, like a bed luring her to come and lie down. She was so happy, so excited.

The sharp waves of water crashed against her back, shattering her bones into a thousand pieces. She felt the water take her in like she was a lost, orphaned child. She could feel the rhythmic beat of her heart slow down. The throbbing in her lungs and head felt so warm. So warm that it felt like a flame was lit inside her. Her chest collapsed in on itself. She began shaking as her body craved oxygen. Nothing mattered anymore. Her last breath left her body. An emotion previously lost in her soul's depths coursed through her veins. All the cuts that lined her stomach, that littered her thighs and arms, felt like they were bleeding once more. Pure fear was running through her mind, and she knew that. But, as her heart went still, as her blood ceased its circulation, she was overwhelmed by one thought. She was free.

Aleia stood behind the mirror, watching everything happening to that little girl. The only difference was that before, the image was only foggy. Now, it was pitch black.

Aiden was pacing around his living room, scared, anxious, and worried that he had done something wrong. He felt like a character for a satirical cartoon who did something stupid and was now facing the consequences. He liked her so much. Scratch that; he loved her so much. Though they'd only known each other for 3 months, he knew almost everything about her emotions. He knew what she was feeling based on her expression, what was running through her mind based on her word choice and tone, and he knew that something happened in the past week. 'What?' was the question.

It seemed like the universe read his mind because one text message, which determined the life of his loved one, made his phone buzz in his hand. He checked his notifications to see that it was from Aleia. Getting infinitely more curious, he hastily opened it. The coursing adrenaline in his veins made it hard to grasp every detail properly, but three phases practically jumped out of the screen to glare at him.

1. 'Thank you'.
2. 'It wasn't your fault'.
3. 'I'll see you in the next life, Aiden. Goodbye'.

He was confused. Aiden felt the gears in his head churning until it finally clicked. Then, his mind went numb. It felt like he was kicked in the stomach and turned to stone.

Everything in his brain and body stopped briefly, and then he ran. Aiden slammed the front door open, not bothering to close it. His mom called after him, yelling with concern. He didn't care. He knew her. He knew Aleia was going to do something drastic. He ran as fast as his legs could take him. He ran with the wind acting as his accelerator. His chest tightened. She never told anyone anything, and the probability that her parents knew something was happening was so goddamn low. She was going to die.

Tears flowed from his eyes as he held back sobs. He was close to her now, only a little bit farther. Aiden wouldn't know what to do if she died. She was the only one who kept him sane and content. He fell in love with how big her heart was, her thought processes, and the purity of her soul. What would he do if her heart no longer pumped blood, if her mind couldn't keep their memories anymore, or if her soul roamed in the skies instead of her body?

In the vicinage, he could see her embellished three-storied house. It was a little small but large enough to be cozy and comfortable. The interiors were decorated with vintage collection pieces, fuzzy carpets, and family portraits. He felt no boredom as Aleia gave him a tour of the whole house. Every time Aiden made her laugh, it felt like a part of him healed. He couldn't lose her. It hurt to know that she hid so much from him to ensure he wasn't worried or hurt. There were dozens of house plants that she watered every alternate day. Would they die along with her? A billion unconventional thoughts filled his head with fear and determination, forcing his legs to move faster.

A small, blue car pulled up to their front porch and parked. Aleia's parents emerged from the car doors, glowing with love and releasing twinkling laughter that livened anyone who heard it. They unlocked the door and were about to step inside. With the velocity and momentum he had while running toward the patio, he almost crashed into them.

"She's," he paused to breathe, "in trouble–"

Mrs Ledger stared at him with bafflement. "Aiden? What–?"

His heart tore at their confusion. He didn't know what to do. How could he possibly tell them their daughter might be dead? Aiden sincerely apologized for his inconvenience and then raced into their home. He navigated his way to Aleia's room and desperately turned the knob to see if it would open. When it didn't, his panic doubled. Aiden could try breaking the door open with brute force; then, he realized that the scenario would end with a dislocated shoulder and an unbroken door. His second option was to pick the lock. He knew he had Bobby Pins in his pockets, but then her parents might question where he learned this, and he did *not* have the time to explain Magic Camp. *'Screw that, Aleia's so much more important.'*

He quickly got to work, maneuvering through the lock and eventually breaking it. The door swung wide open, and the view before him made his body go still. His knees gave in on themselves, and he helplessly crawled to her.

The bottle had rolled out of her hand when she supposedly hit the floor, spilling the rest of its contents. Aiden felt the pills under his palms, triggering another wave of tears. He painfully moved to position himself in a way where Aleia's head was on his lap. Sweat lined her forehead and neck, making a few strands of her hair stick to her skin. He put two fingers to her neck and prayed. His eyes widened when he felt the pulse, which was slow and weak.

Aleia's parents were in the room now, with tears running down their faces, collecting at their chins and dropping to the floor. They were so still that they looked inanimate.

Aiden put one of his shaking hands on her forehead, and the other ungracefully took hold of his phone and called the emergency number.

"Please," he waveringly exhaled, "help."

Chapter 6

"YOU'RE GOING TO BE OKAY"

The snow of yesterday,
That fell like cherry blossoms,
Is water once again,

By Gozan

JANUARY 30ᵀᴴ, 2018

"Beep. Beep. Beep."

Aleia woke up to the rhythmic ring of her alarm. With shut eyes, she tried flailing around to find the snooze button, but then she hit something squishy, so she decided to stop moving when she had no sense of sight. There was a severe pounding in her head, making her feel like someone was bonking her with a hammer. She registered the harsh light that pierced her eyelids, making her close her eyes with more pressure until she only saw beautiful phosphenes. After she knew her pupils had adjusted to the intensity of light, she slowly fluttered them open. She expected to see sunlight filtering through her glass windows, illuminating her room gold; instead, fluorescent bulbs shot down at her. She wasn't in her bed like she usually was. There was no alarm clock or window. The beeping wasn't from a clock shaped like a cat. It was from a medical monitor. IV catheters were coursing liquids into her circulatory system. She wasn't at home. That meant she wasn't dead.

Panic spiked in her mind, simultaneously spiking the frequency of the beeping noises. She was in a hospital room, lying down on her back and loosely gripping a warm hand. As her consciousness came back to her, her headache got exponentially worse. She couldn't sit up either because doing that made her immediately nauseous. However, she got an opportunity to familiarize herself with her surroundings. The stark white walls of the hospital room matched the pristine bedsheets upon which she slept– a plethora of machines beside her pulsed with different colored lights and sounds. IV dripped clear liquid into her numb arms. The hand she held was warm and comforting, but she couldn't make out who it was. A strong scent of disinfectant filled her nostrils, a reminder of the sterile environment she was in. The faint fragrance of hyacinths aromatized the air, likely from a bouquet on her bedside table. With her limited line of sight, she saw the bottom rim of a water jug, which enhanced her excruciating desire for water because she had a parched throat from being unconscious for who knows how long. Tubes and wires were attached to her body, some poking and prodding uncomfortably. The sheets were soft against her skin as she shifted slightly to make out whose hand she was holding. Their intertwined hand felt familiar and comforting, its warmth seeping into her own.

Aleia tried speaking a sentence to the mystery person to ask for water, but due to her fatigue and tight vocal cords, her request came out only as a single word.

She croaked out, "Water?"

Aleia knew the person was startled because their hand quickly unclasped from hers, and then the sound of utter chaos broke loose. She heard the legs of a chair scrape against the floor, a reverberating clang of metal hitting the ground, a loud curse of pain, and clumsy shuffling, till a hopeful face was parallel to her.

She squeaked with surprise due to the sudden intimacy. Then, she realized who it was. She whispered and meagerly pointed to the jug, "Water."

His face flushed when he realized he had forgotten her plea. He hastily filled a glass, and when her aerial view returned, he seemed slightly redder (she didn't think that was possible). It seemed like her questioning expression spoke for her because he promptly muttered, "I spilled a lot of water."

If her skull didn't physically start throbbing every time she laughed, she probably would've been on the floor by now. Aiden redirected the pillows to be leaning against the bedframe and gently propped her up. She gratefully accepted the refreshing liquid. *'You don't deserve this.'*

"Don't you hate me?" she whispered.

His eyebrows furrowed in confusion as he replied, "What on Earth would make you think that? Aleia, I would move a building if it stops you from watching the sunset. I can't actually do that, but it's how much you mean to me. I would hurt anyone that hurts you, but I can't do that now because you hurt yourself." His voice softened, "We were so, *so* scared. I can't lose you. You're the only one wedged so deep in my heart. I feel safe around you; I could show you my silly side, and you'd still be here, probably laughing, but *here*. I don't know what

I would have done if–" she could see tears welling in his eyes "–If you weren't here right now."

'He doesn't care. He's just showing worry because of where I am. He doesn't care.'

Aleia stared at her hands. Tears formed in her eyes. "I'm sorry."

He took her hand, which wasn't connected to the IV, and held it to his heart. "Please, just tell me next time. I'm always here for you."

'That's not true,' she thought. A drop of water hit her hand. Tears escaped Aiden's eyes, and the seriousness of the situation hit her. If he hadn't figured out something was wrong when he did, Aleia would be dead. She would simply be food for worms and fungi. Aleia nodded to his plea, and to that, he swiftly wiped away the salty solution that dampened his face.

She timidly asked him, "How are my parents?"

Aiden looked like he was carefully stringing together a response that accurately depicted the situation but left no one hurt. "They're hurt and scared. They feel so guilty because they think they're responsible for what happened,"

"I guess they didn't read the letter, then?"

He steadily shook his head. "Not yet. Also, you were completely still for a week. You looked like you turned to stone. I'm not sure they even know you're awake, love. They went home to freshen up and get a new pair of clothes. Give them some time. When your parents come back, I'm sure you'll be smothered with hugs. They love you so much, Aleia. They practically took turns camping here, regardless of how exhausted they felt."

Her chest clenched with pain. Aleia wasn't guilty of what she did because it truly felt like the end of the road at the time. The question of 'if' continued to resonate in her head. She wondered what would be happening at this moment if he had not found her. Aiden's words played on a loop in her mind until it stopped on one word.

"Love?"

Aiden burst into flames again. She thinks she spaced out while he rambled on about why he used that nickname, in a flurry of embarrassment, because it felt like she was trapped in a dream. Everything became overly saturated, his voice turned into alluring warbles, and she experienced all her life's emotions cascading, leading up to that one word - love.

The imagery that typically formed in her mind when she visualized information turned static. She was overwhelmed.

A dreamer's mind was one that was oversensitive. She noticed things that most didn't and spent her time overthinking and analyzing every one of her conversations. She often drew gory sketches to represent the pain and fear that went through her head, subsequently creeping people out and pushing them away. But that also meant she had a strong connection between her thoughts and visualization. She had an imagination that would put settings from novels to shame. She had an urge to dream big and often was disappointed when those dreams didn't come to fruition. Her fantasies and idealized visions were what got her through the day. It was all she had when no other part of her felt true. She used to be so optimistic about what her future would bring, but that part of her inner child was immediately crushed when she realized the societal pressure upon her. Not only her, but every kid. They expect you never to show sadness or fear in society, and if you did publicize it, they would promptly tell you to stop. She was expected to keep quiet even if something horrible was happening because being loud was an unattractive trait for a woman. As a child, she was naive, enjoyed having her head in the clouds, and spent most of her time in worlds that didn't exist. As she grew older, her dreams got locked away in a box and shoved under a bed. When she wanted them back, she could no longer reach that box, and with every failed attempt, her desire to live was reduced. Now, she found someone gradually retrieving and protecting her dreams with his heart. She knows she should push him away and ensure he finds someone better, but her heart holds her back.

Aiden cautiously tapped on her shoulder, "Knock, knock."

Aleia snapped back to the present. Aiden had stopped chattering and now looked at her with mild concern. She looked at the boy with affection. She suddenly realized her staggering gratitude for the someone who loved her for all her traits. As a ramification, soft sobs rocked her body, and a combination of joyful and melancholy tears flowed from her eyes.

She felt a warm embrace around her body. Aiden nuzzled his head between her shoulder and neck and placed a hand on her arm to draw arbitrary shapes with the tip of his finger to comfort her. Once she stopped shaking, he pulled away, cupped her face, and lit a flame of hope in her heart. He tenderly whispered, "You'll be okay, love."

CHAPTER 7

THE BLOOM OF FLOWERS

Snowmelt—

On the banks of the torrent,

small flowers

By Penny Harter

MARCH 13TH, 2018

"Just cut all ties with them. It's literally that simple," exclaimed a frustrated Aiden. He was sprawled on her bed, staring up at her slowly rotating fan with a frown.

"Talking to them clearly hurts you, and it can't be easy keeping up a happy facade for people you don't even know, simply because you're afraid of their prejudice."

He looked at Aleia, who was grumpily sitting on the floor of her bedroom, facing the window. Luckily for him, Aiden was parallel to the window, so she was technically turned to him.

She was essentially on lockdown because her mom was paranoid that something would happen before she got in a session with a therapist, and she wanted to be there for Aleia. She couldn't leave the neighborhood; if she did, she must take someone to accompany her. That was the reason a five-foot radius around Aleia became Aiden's second home. She was so lucky to have found someone with a heart as pure as his. She was also reasonably surprised he stood by her even after he realized how disgusting she was. For the past two weeks, she was at her worst, but he never bothered and continued to tend to her (minus the time he was at school, but he still cared about her by telling their classmates she had a horrible cold and then bringing back her classwork).

Aleia observed the birds and trees through the glass barrier. She loved how the wind was becoming less harsh, how the birds began migrating back because the sun started regaining its heat, how they spent their day collecting sticks and hay to build a home, and how buds of flowers littered the branches. The thick leaves of the sassafras tree acted as a mesh, only allowing the most substantial beams of sunlight to pass through to her room. Aleia's voice wavered as she replied, "But then, I'll lose everyone."

The panic-stricken girl felt her tear ducts activate, and it seemed like Aiden noticed because he immediately commented, "You look adorable. Did you know that?"

She let out a wary laugh and turned to lock eyes with Aiden, who had already been gazing at her with warm eyes.

"I'm serious. I'll have no one," she softly whispered.

"Hey, I'm serious too. First of all, you *are* adorable, and second, what do you think I am? A potato?"

Aleia rolled her eyes with amusement. "Okay, other than you."

Since he was rolled on the bed, half his face was smushed against the pillow. So, when he tried showcasing his sarcastic disappointment by repeating "tsk, tsk, tsk," he looked like a baby who had something stuck in his mouth. Aleia giggled.

Aiden looked like he was about to say something mockingly but changed his mind at the last moment. "I know you can make new friends with people who appreciate who you are. You're so kind and take people's boundaries and thoughts seriously. It makes them feel special," he blushed. I mean, at least it makes me feel special."

Aleia raised an eyebrow and smirked. "What are you trying to say, Mr. Castellan?"

He stuffed his face into a cookie-shaped pillow, and before he could respond, a knock came at her already open door. Aiden sat up, and she turned 180° to identify who was there. Confusion flooded her brain when she saw her mom leaning against the frame.

"Aren't you supposed to be at work?" Aleia questioned. She amusingly added, "Also, why are you knocking if the door is already open?"

Her mom smiled and replied to both questions, "I took half the day off, and I knocked to tell you I was here in case you two were doing some unholy things. You weren't, but neither of you noticed me, so I chose to knock anyway."

Both teenagers were burning red. Aiden was entirely hidden by pillows at that point, and Aleia exclaimed, "MOM!"

"Jokes aside," she winked at them. "You have an appointment with Ms. Grace in an hour, so you better start getting ready, sweetie."

An alarm spiked in her heart. '*What if she hates me? What if she thinks my problems are dumb? Oh no. What if she thinks* I'm *dumb?*' Aiden peeked his eyes out from under the bedding and asked if he could drop her off. He stated that he "got used to being around her and would love to be there for her during such an important event."

It's an understatement to say Aleia instantly calmed down.

Aleia's mom paused to think for a bit, then nodded. "I think you can go, but you probably can't stay. All right, both of you, get ready and meet me in ten minutes. It takes about half an hour to get there, but we never know with afternoon traffic. Does that sound good?"

Aleia lightly redid her makeup, threw on a cardigan, and substituted her Mickey Mouse shorts with light blue cargo pants. Aiden stared at himself in the mirror for five minutes, decided nothing was wrong, and then teased Aleia for taking so long. They made their way to the main door, where her mom was waiting for them in the car. Aleia glanced at the kitchen as she passed, noticing the subtle whistle from the kettle, the opened window that let crisp wind enter the room, and the medicine cabinet with its door dislodged from the hook that kept it shut. All of a sudden, a flurry of emotions locked her present mind and sent it back to the day she almost lost her life. Her vision became identical to that of someone with astigmatism. The bright light that flitted through the window suddenly shapeshifted, like a divine figure took each ray and stretched it in twelve directions. A filter of dust seemed to have settled atop the room, causing a desaturating effect on everything she saw. Her peripheral vision closed in on her by the second, causing it to feel like she was trapped in a VR game whose sole purpose was inducing perturbation. Her diaphragm contracted, blocking the passage of air into her lungs. Every sensation, feeling, and thought Aleia felt from the day was vividly reenacted in front of her, yet all she could do was watch. She felt like rapping her fists against the locked mind she was contained in, begging to escape. She lost complete sense of the surroundings of today, and as a juxtaposition, her sentient mind perceived January 20th, the one day she wished to forget, with profuse definition.

She panicked.

Her perspective changed. Aleia could now see her past self walking through each action. She saw tears brimming in her eyes. She saw the rosiness that dusted her cheeks from frustration. She saw her shaking hand reach into the cabinet and retrieve the all-too-familiar container.

She panicked. She couldn't succumb to those thoughts, not again. She knew any trigger would rip the delicate veil she had painfully made to bury everything she felt. She couldn't disappoint her parents again. She couldn't hurt Aiden again, the one friend she had who cared for her beyond the smile she plastered on her face.

She panicked. She saw herself haphazardly making her way to her room. She couldn't move, couldn't stop anything that was about to occur.

Then she felt three taps on her shoulder. The walls that locked her consciousness, the chains that prevented her from moving, and the rapidly building pressure inside her melted away. The relief she felt was tantamount to taking a breath after holding it for what seemed like an eternity.

"Are you okay?" Aiden asked with a worried, single raised eyebrow. She didn't have the heart to answer.

Aleia had her hands pressed against the car seat, taking deep breaths to soothe her anxiety. It didn't seem like it would start raining, but tiny raindrops covered the windows, forming a distorted shield between the roads and the individuals in the car. The drizzle formed tiny rivers on the glass, like intricate roads, leading in different directions.

She decided that breathing didn't help, so she opened half the window to focus on her calming surroundings. The clouds that released the water were still snow-white, making it seem more majestic than stormy. The sun still illuminated the ground, the leaves ever so slightly swayed with the wind, and small animals like rabbits and squirrels ran happily through the dewy, grassy areas. The earthy and fresh petrichor smell mingled with the sweet fragrance of wildflowers from the side of the road, creating a comforting atmosphere. Aleia realized that the weather, which was so lovely, wouldn't come around for another few months, and she knew her mom would forgive her for anything she was about to do because she was going to a literal therapist, so she stuck her head out of the casement.

She did not regret doing that at all. From inside the car, she could hear her mom telling her to 'stop it' and Aiden's whoops of cheer. The rain tasted clean and pristine, as if it had been purified by the clouds it fell from. By comparison, she discovered how stale and stuffy the car was. The slight pitter-patter of raindrops on the car's roof created a soft background noise, almost soothing in its rhythm. She could see each drop splatter as it hit the pavement made of concrete and tar with immense speed. The raindrops were cold against the skin, almost freezing. They left small water trails as they slid into the car from the apertures she created. Among the rain was an invigorating mist and breeze, which made her feel the most alive she had been for the past weeks. In the distance, she could see a marble plaque that read "HOUSE OF HOPE & BLOOM." The cliché name made her a little skeptical, but she was nervous about what awaited nonetheless.

The interior of the building was beautifully decorated. Potted plants littered the waiting room, and soft pastel furniture complemented the overgrown leaves. Rice-white walls circled the room, making it look minimalistic yet comforting. After they registered Aleia's name in the system, her mom briefly met the therapist. Aiden hugged her, and before she went into the room, she simply said, "Wish me luck," with a smile.

***

She came out of that room like a ghost (no, she's not dead yet). Aleia was completely pale after uncomfortably talking about every hardship she ever had, and honestly, she didn't think she would be able to share that freely. The therapist (Aleia learned that her name was Leigha Grace) was unbelievably kind and nurturing, and Leigha said she was open to staying with her for multiple hours if it meant she could get comfortable. The professional never judged Aleia and always listened to what she had to say. She supposes that's what made it okay to talk about her issues and how to move forward with them. However, it took the majority of the first hour to soothe her mind and break her 'never let strangers know your emotions' rule. In the end, Aleia got so much off her chest that she felt like she was floating in the air – like a ghost.

The session went on for quite a while, around four hours, and it was 7:30 PM now. Aleia was patiently waiting outside the building for her dad to come and pick her up. She ecstatically waved when she saw her cute little blue car come around the corner. He always brought this car whenever something discouraging happened to her because he knew how much she loved it. It warmed her heart to see that he still remembered.

After Aleia safely got on, she expected the car to move. It didn't. Then she thought maybe her dad expected more safety, so she strapped her seatbelt. They still didn't move. She stared at her dad with an expectant expression, and with an almost evil grin, he said, "We're not moving till we talk."

She was concerned, to say the least. Aleia turned to face him and softly replied, "What do you want to talk about?"

His countenance morphed from a grin to one that looked like hesitance before rambling, "Everything. How about the fact that I didn't realize my *only* daughter was feeling so terrible that such crude thoughts passed her mind? I'm so sorry. I should have known. Your mom and I should've been there for you. You were going through so much."

Her father looked like he was holding back tears, which provoked the all-too-familiar stinging pain in her chest. "This happened because I hid my feelings from everyone. There's no way you could've known,"

He reached out to gently kiss the top of her head and cleared his throat. "I just want you to be okay,"

A tear dripped down her face, Aleia only noticing it when the droplet hit her palm. She feigned a smile and replied, "I know. It'll take time, but I think I will be." She looked at the scar on her forearm, made from the tubes that supplied life back into her body. Aleia took a quivering breath and continued, "Every memory from that day replays in my mind each time I close my eyes. I feel like I'm living that moment again and again, and that pain is akin to walking on burning coals barefoot." The rate at which the droplets hit her palm increased. "It sucked, Dad, and it still sucks. The emotions I had two months ago reflect those that I have now, and it's obvious that they do because a suicide attempt can't change that." She wasn't sure why her tone changed to one of frustration. "I'll be fine," she exclaimed twice– the former with an inflection of determination and the latter laced with panic.

The air in the small car became heavy with silence, tantamount to the pressure one would feel at the bottom of the ocean. After a moment, Aleia wearily spoke again, "It was only the first session, but Leigha talked about ways I could express what I feel." She meant it as a statement, but it came out as a question. She continued, "She suggested journaling or diary entries, but I don't think that would work for me too effectively. I know I won't be consistent with it unless I know it's helping someone."

Mr Ledger presented a weary smile and opened his mouth to reply in a timid register. When he noticed Aleia's apologetic and guilty expression, he changed his approach to pierce the tension. The characteristics of his face complimented each other to form an overly dramatized look of ponder. His eyes squinted with focus; his chin rested on one of his palms, and his eyebrows furrowed. It looked like a lightbulb lit above his head. "What if you host small sessions teaching younger kids about what you think the biggest problems are? That way, you can enforce awareness, teach them ways to avoid or overcome these issues, and ensure that the upcoming generation won't go through what you did. It'll also help you not let any emotion accumulate *and* it would be helping those children."

Aleia's eyes widened with hope. "That's perfect."

CHAPTER 8

WHAT ONCE FLEW, FLIES AGAIN

The light of a candle

Is transferred to another candle—

Spring twilight.

By Yosa Buson

APRIL 28TH, 2018

Aleia nervously stood in the corner of a classroom filled with thirteen-year-olds. For the past two weeks, she had been preparing content and essentially ranting her mind out every time she got the chance. She knew what it felt like to succumb to judging yourself based on vanity, and with the increasing pressure to adhere to social conventions, it became a thousand times more normal to constantly feel judged for being who you are. Everyone knows that society sets a standard for us to achieve, but is that really worth achieving if it means tearing down our sense of identity?

When her dad gave her the idea, she didn't think it would be so nerve-racking. *'What if I mess these kids up forever? What if I accidentally say something stupid and then they'll blame me for the rest of their lives?'*

She was at her old middle school and asking to conduct a session for the eighth graders was reasonably straightforward. Aleia wanted them to know how pressurizing the world is as they grow, and it would be nice to have a warning before they immediately have to jump into society with no armor. So, that idea gave birth to her most important point: 'Be true to yourself.'

Once the teacher settled them down, she turned off the lights, booted up her presentation, and jumped a few times to calm her nerves. In his words, Aiden was sitting in the back to 'give her moral support and be there to cut awkwardness, if any.' It was comforting to see him there because if she ever got too skittish seeing their doe-eyed looks, Aleia could just look at him, and he'd make a silly face. The introduction started rocky, but once she got around to discussing the issues that mattered, she seemed unstoppable. She spoke of unrealistic expectations, how preserving your identity and building relationships that are based on transparency is vital, how there's immense social stigma around expressing 'sadness' in public, her own story (but made it less explicit), and how knowing and understanding this would help them in the future. By the end, some kids had sympathetic frowns on their faces, some were aggressively nodding in agreement with the points she made, and others looked like they were about to start clapping. Tears were welling in her eyes, and her face was rosy because of how much she talked. The blend of reactions to the end of her speech struck her with anxiety. She wearily searched for Aiden's eyes in hopes of conversing with their minds. He seemed to understand what the poor girl was feeling, immediately giving her a double thumbs-up and walking toward her.

Aleia's preexisting pink cheeks became even rosier when Aiden came to hug her as congrats, and the whole class collectively screamed, 'OooOoOoOO.'

A tide of relief flooded her veins as if a heavy weight had been lifted off her chest. She was incredibly overwhelmed by what she had just accomplished, resulting in a loss of her senses. The gaily chatter of many conversations across the room melded into a hushed hum in her ears, like she was underwater. Her eyes shifted in and out of focus, like a camera lens attempting to focus on a subject in the distance. The subject in question was a small cutout of her middle school mascot, pinned on a blackboard at the very back of the wall as a symbol of recovery from the painful path she had chosen to walk. The lingering buzz from the session filled her with pride and disbelief that she had actually pulled it off. Simultaneously, she couldn't believe how much 'talking about it' positively and beneficially freed up something tight and constricting inside her. Her mind felt partly light for the first time in months, as if she had regained the potential to fly and dream. She bid a short goodbye to the students, promising them she'd return after extraordinary pleading from their side once her parents came to pick her up. Their eyes twinkled with curiosity as they exchanged glances and talked inaudibly to the teacher.

Their tete-a-tete was embellished with nodding and smiles. Aleia was out of earshot, but she knew it was a conversation full of reassurance– everything had gone just fine. As she was getting close to mastering reading their lips, she was snapped out of focus by a tap on her shoulder.

Aiden told her that he was going home because, apparently, his mom called to remind him of his forgotten promised plans that the boy made with her. She playfully chastised him about their lack of time together, especially now that he was going to college, and stated that she would 'take away his TV privileges if he didn't go back this instant'.

She insisted her parents wouldn't mind dropping him home, but he apprehensively laughed and told her he loved the weather so much that he simply couldn't miss out. She glanced out the window toward the heavy sheet of gray over the sky and turned back to him with a raised eyebrow. She knew the wind was too sharp to find it enjoyable, but anyone could've spotted the zeal in his eyes, so she laughed and bid him goodbye. Later, Aiden confessed that he didn't know whether his mom would come running out throwing slippers at him or give him a bone-crushing hug, and he didn't want to handle the embarrassment in front of her parents.

On the drive home, the interrogation started.

She was sitting in the back, so her mom turned her head from the front and eagerly looked at Aleia like a gossip-deprived teenager. When he got the chance between driving, her dad looked at her from the rear-view mirror.

Her mom started, "So," she paused, "did you like it?" Aleia exuberantly nodded.

It instantly prompted her second question, "Do you think this is helping you? If so, we're here to give you everything you need."

Aleia smiled at her enthusiasm. "Yeah, I feel much better now. It feels good to know that what you're doing could help someone. I finally understand why you put so much effort into your work, Mom."

They were at a red light. Her father briefly turned to ask her, "Do you think you'd want to do this again?"

Despite her promise, she wasn't sure. She had fun, but what if she gave them everlasting impressions about right and wrong? Aleia knew she was qualified to talk to them and even went over her content with her school counselor, but the irrational fear of something going haywire daunted her. Cutting off all her ties with people she had 'relationships' with was what truly freed her, but the only reason she's okay is because she has someone who loves her infinitely more than her friends' liking combined. She wouldn't give the children such harmful advice because she knew how it could affect them, so her mind came to a jittering halt.

When her heart had a counter-argument for every anxiety-induced thought, she timidly nodded 'yes.'

They smiled brightly at her. "That's truly amazing, sweetie. I hope you know we're so willing to support you in any way. We want you to be happy, and I don't want you to force a smile around us ever again, Aleia. Also, the talk with the teacher was fairly insightful. She said the response with her kids was better than she had ever seen to a guest speaker. Ms. Locke informed us she would be happy to see if other classes would like you to talk to them as well. I know I also speak for your dad when I say you should sleep on the idea, at the least."

Aleia's jaw dropped to the floor; out of surprise or excitement, she wasn't sure.

Her dad chuckled, "We're really proud of you, Lea. Though you may not admit or know it yet, we know you'll be genuinely good at it."

Her mom lovingly added, "Worst case, we can always say something came up and ghost the teacher for the rest of time. You're strong, and if you choose to pursue this, I know you'll excel."

She felt her hands jitter with adrenaline. For the first time in a long time, she had something big to look forward to. She had a goal that she could follow. She could dream.

***

SEPTEMBER 1ST, 2018

She rested her head against the side of her bed while she stared into the sky beyond her window. Golden rays of light streaked through the pink hues of sunset. The white clouds starkly contrasted the atmosphere's ombre of color. Beyond the sassafras tree, Aleia could see crows soar through the sky, having the wind as their ally. It was a perfect end to the day.

A sketchbook lay still on her lap, her fingers loosely wrapped around a pencil. She flipped through old pages of the book, staring at the shabby lines she drew with frustration and fear. The image on the paper was so raw that it felt like she was living through that again.

Aleia flipped back. Now, she often sketched things that reminded her of what she loved, like Aiden, her parents, and pretty little flowers. It warmed her heart to see how much she had changed.

Her room was showered only with light from the outdoors as she closely watched the pigments that colored the air become more intense. Birds chirped in the distance, and she could hear the faint rustle of leaves, but it all felt so serene.

Aleia looked at Aiden as he slowly entered, and he looked golden in the room's glow. There was no noise, no disturbance. He took a seat on the cold marble floor next to her.

He whispered, "What's up?"

A smile automatically graced her when she heard his voice. "I'm not sure anymore. Daydreaming, I guess."

Aiden teasingly replied, "You've got so many dreams that they happen during the day now, huh?"

She put her hand in his, their fingers interlocking. "I'm just happy."

EPILOGUE

The west wind whispered,

And touched the eyelids of spring,

Her eyes, primroses.

by R.M. Hansard

NOVEMBER 21ST, 2018

She was excited for today. It was the one day people could compliment her, and she would feel no guilt. She wore a pretty baby-pink dress with simplistic sandals and a gold necklace. It was definitely not as grand as her celebration from last year, but she was a thousand times happier.

A large chunk of the party occurred in her living room because no more than twenty people were invited. After everything she went through in the last year, she firmly held her stance on not asking people to come to her birthday party unless she knew them by heart. Both her parents and Aiden wholeheartedly agreed. A tiny pile of gifts accumulated on the couch, each carefully wrapped with pristine paper. Helium balloons floated in the air from clusters tied down with a pebble. Many of those who escaped their grounding ended up bouncing against the ceiling. Her mom's homemade food lined a table, filling the room with the savory scent of pasta and garlic bread. Everything had changed, but she knew it had changed for the better. Over the past 6 months, she made friends who genuinely loved her, something she never thought possible. Her past self would've been surrounded by foreign faces, but now, she was surrounded by people who knew her, accepted her, and loved her for who she was. Through it all, one person remained constant. At the center of her heart stood Aiden, who was currently laughing with some of her friends. She couldn't believe he stood by her even after the pain she put him through.

Pop music played on the speakers connected to her dad's phone, and the song was interrupted by her mom's shush. She quieted down the chatter and the music, and dramatically said, "It's the time you've all been waiting for!"

Her mom stood at the front of the living room, holding a large cake. She had a dramatic flair for these kinds of announcements, and after eighteen years of going through them, Aleia's embarrassment had significantly reduced. Her father rolled his eyes playfully and Aiden bounced up and down with excitement.

The lights turned off, plunging the room into darkness, and the only illumination was from a cluster of candles on a heart-shaped cake. The subtle scent of vanilla and butter wafted through the air. It was frosted, lined with white buttercream, and carefully decorated with big white pearls and pink sprinkles. Her mom continued, "Everyone, huddle around. Dear, record it, would you?" she asked her husband. He reached for the camera, ready to capture the moment on video.

Aleia took in the sight of everyone gathered around the table, their faces illuminated by the candlelight and genuinely seeming like they were eager to be there for her. A sense of contentment washed over her, and she was grateful she hung onto these small, cherished moments that made life worth living. Her mom put the cake on the table, hugged Aleia, and told her, "You deserve this, sweetie."

Pure elation erupted inside her. She felt like the Grinch when his heart grew three sizes. It had been so long since she felt so special, with no small voice telling her she was selfish.

When they began singing, she cut the cake and made a wish, blowing out the candles in one big breath. Tears formed in her eyes, and she didn't even realize it. The day was perfect. She relished her parents' hands on hers as she sliced through the pastry, the gaiety aura that emitted from her friends, and the soft peck Aiden placed on her cheek (followed by a dollop of frosting).

They cheered together, "HAPPY BIRTHDAY!"

Aiden attacked her with a bear hug and wished her again, as if he hadn't done that a dozen times throughout the day. In his arms, her heart bloomed with felicity, and her lips turned to form a benign smile. She finally felt happy, with no loopholes or 'buts'.

Here she was, encompassed by nothing but love and rapture. They were the ones who allowed her to hope and dream. The kind of hope that brings a withered rose to life, even after the harshest winter. Aleia was no longer caged. She was home.

ABOUT THE AUTHOR

Niharika Bodla is a budding author who has developed a strong passion for writing and languages over the years. With a keen eye for detail and a deep observation of the societal pressures to maintain appearances, she has channeled her thoughts and emotions into the creation of this novella.

From a young age, reading provided her with an escape into worlds beyond her own, nurturing her imagination and creativity. This love for literature, paired with innate talent, evolved into a passion for writing, offering her a space to express herself authentically and without judgment. Through her writing, Niharika aspires to connect with readers on a profound level, sharing stories that resonate with their experiences, observations, or emotions.